Phoebe and Her Unicorn

Phoebe and Her Unicorn

Dana Simpson

Andrews McMeel
PUBLISHING®

INTRODUCTION

i would dearly love to claim at least some connection to the origins of Marigold Heavenly Nostrils, the innocently arrogant unicorn who preens so charmingly through Dana Simpson's delightful comic strip bearing her name. And perhaps I can. Scholarly articles have been written, after all, about the fact that prior to my 1968 novel *The Last Unicorn* there were no female unicorns to be found in any of the world's varied mythologies. And in the early pages of that book I did write "Unicorns are immortal. It is their nature to live alone in one place: usually a forest where there is a pool clear enough for them to see them-selves—for they are a little vain, knowing themselves to be the most beautiful creatures in all the world, and magic besides . . ."

A little vain . . . Marigold would be an appalling monster of ego, utterly self-concerned and completely unlikable, if it weren't for her sense of humor and her occasional surprising capacity for compassion—both crucial attributes when bound by a wish granted to a nine-year-old girl in need of a Best Friend to play invented superhero games with, to introduce to slumber parties and girl-talk gossip and to ride through the wind after being called nerd and Princess Stupidbutt one time too many. For Phoebe is a remarkably real little girl, as bright and imaginative as Bill Watterson's Calvin, as touchingly vulnerable as Charles Schulz's Charlie Brown. And if these strike you as big names to conjure with, I'll go further and state for the record that in my opinion *Phoebe and Her Unicorn* is nothing less than the best comic strip to come along since *Calvin and Hobbes*. Simpson is that good, and that original.

Part of the charm of *Phoebe and Her Unicorn* is the way in which Simpson plays her two characters' opposed world views—immortal and contemporary— against each other, along with their egos: for Phoebe's determination to be recognized as Awesome quite matches Marigold's impregnable superiority to the entire human species. Consequently, both delight in sticking the needle in where they can, and on this ground they are equals. There is real affection between them, but it grows by degrees. Simpson takes her time with this, always remaining in full control of her material, including artful cultural references and the gradual development of additional characters and themes.

The temptation is to quote at least every gag and panel, but that would be wrong. Enchantment doesn't retail well at secondhand; like Robert Frost's definition of poetry, it gets lost in translation. I'll simply suggest that you go read *Phoebe and Her Unicorn* in a serious hurry.

Like now!

— Peter S. Beagle
Oakland, California
September 2013

7

Tomorrow at show and tell, I'll stand up and say "allow me to present *MY BEST FRIEND, MARIGOLD HEAVENLY NOSTRILS!*"

That's the cue for you to take a flying leap through the window, trailing rainbows and stars!

dana

There may be something wrong with you.

I need you to *SHINE.* I brought some glitter and "Crisco"...

The following day

Show and tell!

First up for show and tell, we have Phoebe!

ahem I have something REALLY REALLY REALLY special and important!

You should SERIOUSLY be sitting down for this.

...

Um, good. Carry on.

THERE you are!

You were supposed to leap into the classroom so everyone could see you and be jealous of me!

SERIOUSLY?

My beauty has transfigured this puddle into a thing of magnificence.

I guess I wanted other kids to think I was special. It's lonely being overlooked.

It is lonely being special, too.

Unicorns are rare. I spend most of my time alone, gazing into crystal pools.

dana

So we're NOT so different!

I am going to pretend I did not hear that.

I don't get it. I brought a *UNICORN* to show and tell, and I'm no more popular than before.

Oh, it is probably the SHIELD OF BORINGNESS.

The shield of boringness?

No, no. The SHIELD OF BORINGNESS.

The shield of boringness.

I will forgive your accent.

dana

Never had a dream before that didn't fade away

Never had a unicorn to ask me out to play

Never had a child with me to share the best of things

A princess of suburbia who dances, laughs and sings

Never was a part of two who run beneath the stars

Never had a someone who could tell me

"THIS IS OURS."

Never be alone again neither day nor night

A princess and a unicorn have finally got it right.

It is your turn to gossip. Tell me something scintillating!

Tommy stuck Dakota's green eraser in his armpit, and she didn't want it back!

I don't know what the word you said means.

That may only be one of many problems.

CRIME IN THIS CITY **NEVER RESTS.**

SO NEITHER DOES...

CLAUSTROPHOEBEA!

TONIGHT SHE IS CALLED UPON TO FACE HER MOST *MENACING, BEASTLY FOE...*

POINTYHEAD.

I have brought you a **COOKIE!**

See? I *KNEW* you'd stink at being the bad guy.

Well, give me back the cookie then.

49

G'night, kiddo.

Say goodnight to my unicorn!

Goodnight, Phoebe's unicorn.

No, no, no. Address her PROPERLY.

Say "may pixies sing you to sleep, o princess of ethereal wonderfulness, light and candy."

I

NO!

If we get some pixies started singing, they will sing until we are driven MAD!!

Then just "g'night, Marigold."

This is it, Marigold.

This'll be the summer I'm big enough and brave enough to jump from the **HIGH** rock.

...Marigold?

Here I am!

I am ready for swimming!

FWIP FWIP FWIP

HEE HEE HEE HEE

HA HA HA HA AAAAA

Do my fins and snorkel clash?

BEST SUMMER EVER!

Mom says they were called "Sugar Kabooms" when she was a kid, but now people have to delude themselves into thinking everything's healthy.

I declare our slumber party complete, and a success!

And I have to say, it may be my greatest achievement yet!

MINE is still the time I discovered the color blue.

Nobody before you had ever seen a blue thing?

Not that **I** had heard about.

plink

Pawns don't move that way.

That one is PAWNGELICA, THE MAGICAL PRINCESS WHO ROAMS THE BOARD.

You made that up.

dana

Maybe you should be my sidekick! Every great detective needs one.

Maybe *YOU* should be *MY* sidekick.

All right, we'll settle this democratically.

Excellent!

All in favor of Marigold being the sidekick, raise your hands!

I used to have an elephant pencil topper!

It disappeared last month under **MYSTERIOUS CIRCUMSTANCES.**

THAT'S what we'll investigate.

Any leads?

I suspect it's the work of my **ARCH ENEMY.**

You have an arch enemy?

I must, or where's my pencil topper?

You posted this photo online.

I can CLEARLY see an elephant pencil topper on your desk, JUST like the one I mysteriously lost.

So?

So, this is the part where my brilliant detective work makes you fold like origami!

You're weird.

And YOU'RE doing this wrong!

She is upset!

You **ZAPPED HER HAIR OFF.**

That is a big deal?

YES!

You humans are *MOSTLY* bald anyhow. I did not know you cared so much for what little hair you have.

I...can actually kinda see your logic, but...

What is a tiny bit of extra pink in a sea of fleshy human disgustingness?

Remember what I said about knowing when to stop talking?

She was headed into the park!

Let's split up and meet on the far side of the pond.

Let me see your phone.

ZZAP!

By establishing a magical link to your phone, I will be able to send you text messages!

Unicorns have magic texting powers?

The invention of cell phones has made it much more useful.

I'll need you to SHIELD YOUR EYES as I perform the UNICORN SUMMONING RITUAL.

Come over here now

You're just texting.

I SAID to shield your eyes.

Dakota's shock at losing her hair has distorted the SHIELD of BORINGNESS into something FAR worse...

Dakota, Marigold says she can fix your hair.

Meh.

Something must be done! The **VORTEX OF MEH**, if not stopped, will spiral out of control!

Do you understand what a disaster that would BE for the world?

Meh.

You SEE?

Eep! We gotta DO something!

I guess since you're friends with a unicorn, I won't call you "Princess Stupidbutt" anymore.

Thanks.

Also, thanks for never thinking of "Feeble Phoebe."

Or "Dweeby Phoebe."

You two are killing me here.

Dakota may be unpleasant...

But, like you, she has now seen past the SHIELD of BORINGNESS.

Now, all our destinies are entwined...

FOREVER.

Forever?

Or just for a while. It is not an exact science.

One who has beheld a unicorn, only to feel rejected, can become quite dangerous indeed.

So, next month, I have to let Dakota ride me into her birthday party.

Oh, but I'M not invited, is that it?

You ARE invited.

How come I have to go?

I am detecting ambivalence.

You did not tell your father that the friend you are bringing home is a unicorn.

I doubt he'd have believed me.

I haven't had many friends, and you're a pretty unusual *KIND* of friend.

The kind who lets you sit on her.

My previous friends have *NOT* been cool with that.

Hey, kiddo. And Marigold. Nice to see you again.

Dad, meet my friend, Marigold Heavenly Nostrils!

Charmed.

Why have your parents not offered me moonbeam nectar yet?

She's house-broken, right?

Yeah, this was a brilliant idea.

And THAT is my entire list of ways you should be cooler.

Isn't that right, Marig—

Where'd Marigold go?

Your mother wanted to paint her.

MOM, GIVE me back my UNICORN!!!

I'm secretly cool.

Hurry, Stormchaser! We must find the ORB of FRIENDLINESS before Cacophany does!

You look pensive.

This is the first time I've ever played Pastel Unicorns with an actual unicorn.

It's sort of... I don't know...

Multi-layered?

High-pressure.

dana

My parents seem to like you.

I know. Aren't you delighted?

You don't HAVE parents, do you?

Not that I have ever noticed.

I thought you WANTED your parents to approve of me.

That is why I have been gradually turning down the SHIELD of BORINGNESS all evening.

Briefly it was the SHIELD of ANNOYANCE, because I forgot to carry a five...

It was the SHIELD of HUMORING A CHILD, and then the SHIELD of MILD INTEREST, and then the SHIELD of EYEBROW-RAISING NOVELTY.

I do that sometimes.

Summer vacation's almost over, and I feel like it just started!

Did I even do ANY of the fun stuff I planned to do?

You spent the whole summer riding on the back of a magical unicorn.

All in all, a pretty successful summer!

Except for that huge slug you stepped on barefoot.

Ow!

Hold still if you want to look good for your friend's party.

Dakota is NOT my friend.

Well, you still want to look nice, right?

I want the SIGHT of me to fill Dakota with **EXISTENTIAL DREAD.**

A French braid MAY not do the trick.

Could you get out those plastic Halloween vampire fangs?

dana

Why does nobody seem all that impressed?

I tried to tell you. It is the SHIELD of BORINGNESS.

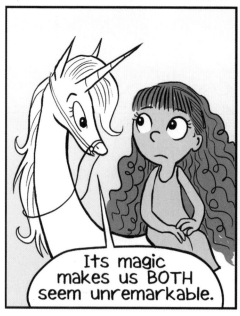

Its magic makes us BOTH seem unremarkable.

I'm not unremarkable! I'm the BIRTHDAY GIRL!

If you wanted to be noticed, you should not have ridden in on a unicorn.

What happened with Dakota?

I am not speaking to her.

Which ALONE would be tragic for her, as I am scintillating.

Does that mean "high-maintenance"?

Dakota wanted what ALL humans want at first.

She wanted to use my radiant specialness to make HERSELF look good.

When I would not help, she called me "pointless."

Poor choice of words.

I am VERY proud of my pointiness.

I was there every day for nine months, and I'll walk past the door every day for the NEXT nine...

My old classroom will have OTHER kids in it.

But I'll **NEVER GO IN AGAIN.**

Do you have a point?

Nope, that's you.

Dr. Phoebe scans for evidence of ancient civilizations.

She combs the desk for signs of fourth-graders who have been here in years past.

Signs point to a king, in the age of metal.

A ruler referred to here as OZZY.

151

BRRRRRINNGG

The first bell of the school year is always the hardest.

i already have to take a SPELLING TEST.

then I'm gonna be assigned a SPELLING PRACTICE PARTNER.

i'll be forced to spend time with some kid I BARELY KNOW.

No comment.

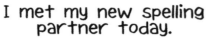
I met my new spelling partner today.

How did it go?

Great!

I...borrowed his glasses without asking, and then demanded he spell my name.

So NOT great.

Kind of dreadful, yeah.

THE NEXT DAY...

inner unicorn
inner unicorn
inner unicorn

Ready to practice spelling?

PFFBTHT

Awesome.

Gimme! I bet I can spit even further.

Unicorns are one thing. Boys are another.

The verb "to fall" means tumbling down
Like in the mud, right on my face

A "fall," the noun, can mean a thing
of beauty, but, for heaven's sake

I didn't know your tail could do that.

I am even more amazing than we realized!

Or falling rain, that makes my world
A muddier and wetter place.

Just watch your hooves, because a fall
can be a tragic thing to take.

But when the leaves are red and gold
the wind is cool, the shadows tall

I celebrate the upper case
delighting in the air of Fall.

I have a piano lesson after school.

I'll be done with school, except WAIT! Instead of freedom, here's MORE school.

Just when I thought I was out, they pull me back in!

Is that a line from something?

Yeah, probably.

dana

The northwestern white-butted unicorn, *caelestis naribus*. A rare find.

Note the smugness of her expression, the superior air of her body launguage, the way even the curve of her tail suggests a smirk.

Let's observe her.

Since when do YOU know Latin?

I don't have to know anything. I have a phone.

Well, my piano teacher doesn't glare at me for not practicing, anymore.

Now he just thinks I'm **stupid**.

AS IF.

Although I did let you manipulate me into playing the piano with my face.

It was hilarious.

In times of yore, record stores were repositories of culture and style.

YOU seem to acquire and play music on that small plastic square.

As a younger human, you may have trouble appreciating a record store properly.

GET OFF MY LAWN, YOU KIDS!

I happen to know **your** lawn is delicious.

I missed the point again.

Indeed.

183

Did you plan that?

Plan what?

You just **HAPPEN** to take me to a record store, where we just **HAPPEN** to find my piano teacher's album.

Are you trying to trick me into learning something?

I would say you think too much of me, if that were possible.

dana

Hear now, for this has been foretold.

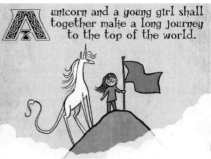

A unicorn and a young girl shall together make a long journey to the top of the world.

Standing at the pinnacle, the girl shall hold aloft a magic talisman.

And thus shall she dip her hand into the river of all knowledge.

How can I still have no signal all the way up HERE?

The prophecy we made up this morning has almost but not quite come true!

dana

189

Could you take me to collect candy where YOU live?

That is acceptable.

Yay!

Your other friends will get to find out what an awesome human you hang out with now!

We will have to find you a **VERY** good disguise.

"Costume."

What are we doing HERE?

You texted me, asking me to bring you **MOUNTAINS**.

An impossible request, but one worthy of a princess.

So I have done the next best thing...

And brought you *TO* the mountains!

I texted you to bring me my MITTENS.

At least I THINK I...

STUPID AUTOCORRECT.

Nice view, anyway.

RAR. RAR RAR RAR RAR RAR.

RAR.

Just make with the candy, Todd.

dana

Hey...

That's my spelling partner Max. He looks sad.

Hey, Max. What's wrong?

People don't believe me that I'm in costume.

That's stupid. You're CLEARLY Steve Jobs.

THANK you.

C'mon. I have enough candy that I can share.

People who DO get it think it's funny to give me apples.

SOMEbody ate all MY apples already.

What is this about someone back there having more apples?

Mom, I can't go to school today! I'm sick!

You look fine.

It's a MENTAL illness.

I've gone CRAAAAAAZY.

Apparently, crazy people still have to go to school.

Even the crazy need not be stupid.

All the other leaves have given up, but that one has **TENACITY.**

It doesn't care that it's different, or that it's alone. It inspires me.

I'm not going anywhere as long as it doesn't!

Except for right now, just really quick.

Where are you going?

Tenacity is easier when you have mittens.

I'm back!
Did the
leaf...

213

How to Draw Marigold

Marigold's head has a circle at the center of it.

Before I draw her unicorny features, she kind of looks like a dinosaur.

Eyes are ovals spaced about one eye apart

Horn has four spiral lines

Her horn is just above her eyes.

(In the very first strips, I wasn't super consistent about this, and she kind of had Wandering Horn Syndrome.)

The front part of her mane is basically a swoop, and is on the far side of her head and horn no matter which way she's facing.

(It's magic.)

A few lines to show her hair's not a solid object

eyes have little highlight dots

little heavenly nostrils

Marigold is kind of swan-shaped, with a long slender neck.

Her body is based on two circles

"shoulder"

←"elbow"

←"wrist"

"knee"→

"ankle"→

Her legs have the same joints as your arms and legs, just arranged a little differently.

Her hooves are cloven (two-pointed), like a deer's. Also she has fluffy fetlocks.

How to Draw
Phoebe

Phoebe's head is very round.

She has oval eyes and a little point for a nose.

Her hair has a lot of lines in it.

She usually, but not always, wears a ponytail.

Eyes have little highlight dots

Freckles!

Missing a tooth!

Her body is also based on two circles

Four fingers, four toes, like a lot of cartoon characters

Unlike some cartoon characters, Phoebe wears different outfits on different days.

Try some! You're holding a whole book of references. Or make up your own!

Make a Marigold Heavenly Nostrils Stick Puppet

MATERIALS: white cardboard or white paper plate; scissors; pencil; large craft stick; markers; glue; tape; yarn

INSTRUCTIONS:

 Photocopy or trace the picture of Marigold, below.

 Color the picture with markers.

 Cut out the picture and glue it on the cardboard or paper plate.

Cut the cardboard or paper plate around the picture.

 Tape the picture to the craft stick.

 Glue yarn for mane.

Make an Animated Flip Book

Cartoonists create stories in cartoon panels. Often cartoonists are also animators. An animator must capture a broad range of movements in order for a cartoon to look continuous. Animation is possible because of a phenomenon called "persistence of vision," when a sequence of images moves past the eye fast enough, the brain fills in the missing parts so the subject appears to be moving.

MATERIALS: paper, index cards, or sticky notes; stapler and staples, paper clips, or brads; pencil or marker

INSTRUCTIONS:

 Cut at least 20 strips of paper to be the exact same size, or use alternative materials, such as index cards or sticky notes.

 Fasten the pages together with a staple, brad, or paperclip.

 Pick a subject—anything from a bouncing ball to a running Marigold or a shooting star.

 Draw three key images first: the first on page one, the last on page twenty, and the middle on page ten, then fill in the pages between the key images.

Make Unicorn Slumber Party Snack Mix

Marigold's favorite food might be luscious, tender grass, but snack mix is required at a slumber party! This is a yummy, easy-to-make treat.

INGREDIENTS: 1 bag Bugles (they look just like unicorn horns!), 1 bag cheddar fish crackers, 1 bag round pretzels, 1 cup nuts (either cashews or peanuts), 1 package ranch salad dressing mix, ½ cup vegetable oil

INSTRUCTIONS:

 Mix the vegetable oil with the dressing mix in a small bowl.

 Put the Bugles, crackers, pretzels, and nuts in a large bowl.

 Add the dressing mixture to the large bowl and mix.

 Store in airtight container or storage bags.

Fun Things to Know About Unicorns

Even though the unicorn is a fictitious animal, it is one of the official animals of Scotland and was used on the royal coat of arms of Scotland in medieval times. (The red lion shown in the shield on the crest is the other official animal.)

Lake Superior State University (through its Department of Natural Unicorns of the Unicorn Hunters) issues Questing Unicorn Licenses. Check it out at:

www.lssu.edu/banished/uh_license.php.

Unicorns have appeared in folklore and art since ancient times in such different places as China, Greece, and France. One of the most famous depictions of unicorns is the *The Hunt of the Unicorn*, a series of seven tapestries that is in The Cloisters, which is part of The Metropolitan Museum of Art in New York. You can see them and learn more about them at:

www.metmuseum.org/collections/search-the-collections/467642.

Create Your Own Cartoon Strip

The comic strip *Phoebe and Her Unicorn* began when Phoebe met Marigold and they became friends. Think about how you met one of your favorite friends and draw a comic strip about it.

MATERIALS: blank piece of paper, pencil, markers, or colored pencils

INSTRUCTIONS:

 1   Make three blank cartoon panels.

 2   Look at the example above to see how Dana Simpson set the stage for the meeting and ended with the punch line.

 3   Once you have decided on the story you want to tell, draw it in three panels. Remember, it should have a beginning, a middle, and an end.

 4   In the first panel, give your comic strip a name.

"We'll be friends forever, won't we, Pooh?" asked Piglet. *"Even longer,"* Pooh answered.
—Winnie the Pooh

Andrews McMeel Publishing
a division of Andrews McMeel Universal
1130 Walnut Street, Kansas City, Missouri 64106

www.andrewsmcmeel.com

18 19 20 21 22 SDB 17 16 15 14 13

ISBN: 978-1-4494-4620-8

Library of Congress Control Number: 2013957200

Made by:
Shenzhen Donnelley Printing Company Ltd.
Address and location of manufacturer:
No. 47, Wuhe Nan Road, Bantian Ind. Zone,
Shenzhen China, 518129
13th Printing—7/16/18

ATTENTION: SCHOOLS AND BUSINESSES

Check out more *Phoebe and Her Unicorn*

If you like Phoebe, look for these books!

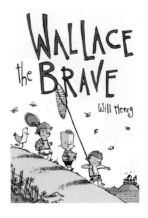